earth warp

Based on the TV scripts by David Angus

Roy Apps

Published by BBC Educational Publishing,
a division of BBC Education,
Woodlands, 80 Wood Lane, London W12 0TT

First published 1994
© Roys Apps/BBC Education 1994

The moral right of the author has been asserted.

Illustrations © Chris Price 1993
Cover illustration © Nick Jordan 1993
Cover and book design by Mark Riches

0 563 35401 1

Set in Stone Informal 11/16

Printed in England by Clays Ltd, St Ives plc

Contents

A note from the past

Albert Dickens stared at the circle of shiny, black prunes in the bottom of his bowl and tried to will them to disappear. He hated hotel breakfasts. He hated hotels. In particular he hated the Burlington Hotel, Southbeach. His father had chosen it for their holiday because it was the newest and most modern one in the town. But there were no other children staying in the Burlington Hotel. There was nothing to *do*. Albert called it the *Boring*-ton Hotel.

'Ha!' grunted Albert's father to no one in particular. He looked up from his newspaper. 'Says here that a German cove name of Herr Otto Lillenthal has got himself killed trying to *fly*! Silly fool thing to do if you ask me. Should've known better.'

Albert looked out of the window. The sun was beginning to burn through the early sea mist. 'One day,' he said, 'there will be huge flying machines in the sky and people will go to the moon.'

Mr Dickens leaned back in his chair and laughed so loud the other guests in the breakfast room all turned round to look.

'Just who fills your head with such nonsense old chap, I do not know, but you'd do well to go for a long walk along the beach to clear your mind. I'm taking my bicycle and going up river to do a spot of fishing.'

The sun shone brightly that summer's morning in 1894. Mr Dickens stood at the water's edge, watching his float bob up and down on the surface of the ice-clear river. A skylark sang high above the meadows that stretched out behind him towards the Downs. But then Mr Dickens became aware of another sound. A sort of whining drone. He spun round, convinced that one of those new-fangled motor carriages was making its way towards him.

So he didn't see the object, about the size of a large boulder, but pinkish and curved like a giant sea shell, drop out of the sky into the river. But he did feel the cold water as it splashed over his head. He didn't bother to hang about to find out what had dropped into the river. He rode straight back to the hotel to change his clothes, explaining to fellow guests – and to a highly amused Albert – that he had slipped and fallen into the river.

The curious shell-like object was well camouflaged, nestling amongst the reeds towards the middle of the river. Indeed it could have been mistaken for a shell, except for the fact that two lights glowed through a crack that stretched halfway round its rim. It would have been a waste of breath to have explained to Mr Dickens that it was only a space probe – an exploratory computerised inter-planetary space capsule sent to earth by an alien life form on the planet Gia. He wouldn't have believed you. After all, he didn't even believe in aeroplanes.

But space capsule it was.

And space capsule it stayed.

Time passed.

As farmland gave way to factories and horse and cart gave way to car, the space capsule settled into the stream and waited, regularly sending back signals and data to the planet Gia.

Until…

…One hundred years later, almost to the day, the Director of Inter-Planetary Research and Exploration on the planet Gia decoded the latest signals from the space probe. Immediately all computer screens at the Inter-Planetary Research and Exploration centre flashed up the words TRHYU GOGZOOG!!

Which, roughly translated into English means: RED ALERT: PLANET EARTH.

This is what happened in
Southbeach during one week
in August last year.
I was there. I made
notes in my diary. This
is my story.

Signed,
Martin Rowlands

1 Day one minus one

S·O·U·T·H·B·E·A·C·H
GAZETTE
— 20th AUGUST · 1993 —

SOUTH BEACH FLOWER AND PRODUCE SHOW
**SHOCK RESULT
IN
LEEK CONTEST!!**
BY
SARAH BRIGHTLY

Neither of them looked up. So I knew they hadn't
seen me. They stood on the bridge yak-yakking away
to each other. I knew them both from school. Jennifer
Steel and Amina Sondhi. Nitro-Jen and Ammonia I
call them. I've got names for everybody.

I don't know why they had come up to this bit of
the river. It's by the boat yard, where the river does a
big kink. And the elbow bit of the kink is really great.
People dump all their junk here. You can find all
sorts of stuff – bottles, prams, fridges – I even found
an old bike once. In fact, Ammonia was gawping at

the present collection of junk: a bashed-in fridge, a
pram with three wheels and a vacuum cleaner with
no handle.

'How can people do that?'

Easy, I thought. You just reverse your car off the
road, take whatever it is out of the boot, heave-ho
and then – splash.

'It's disgusting.'

I sighed. Disgusting is Ammonia's favourite word. Our year head Miss Craddock's cigarettes, Shaun Goacher's pet rat, the Southbeach Burger Bar's hamburgers – they've all been called disgusting by Ammonia.

'It was probably a nice stream once. Look at it now!'

Actually Ammonia had a point. It was pretty grotty out there midstream – cloudy and murky. When the current was strong, it would foam up in scummy bubbles all around the bits of junk.

Nitro-Jen was nodding in agreement with Ammonia as always. I was going to wait for them to go and then go down to get the broken vacuum cleaner. I thought the motor might still be in it. I was *going* to. And then...

And then I found I couldn't get my breath. My chest felt as if someone had dropped an iron bar onto it. I gulped and panted and wheezed. I scrambled around in my jacket pocket for my inhaler and shoved it into my mouth. Stupid. Stupid asthma. Stupid. Stupid inhaler.

Nitro-Jen saw me first – probably heard me wheezing.

'Martin? Martin! Are you all right?'

Stupid asthma. Stupid inhaler. Why did *they* have

to see me like this?

'Go…away…!' I panted.

'Ooh, thank you for asking.' Ammonia thought she was being really sarcastic. She was. So I didn't answer.

I lurched along the road towards the town and home. Tripped.

'Martin! Are you sure you're going to manage to get home?'

'Leave him Jenny, he's OK really.'

Inhale. Deep breath.

'Well he doesn't look OK. Martin, we'll give you a hand.'

Inhale. Deep breath. Push off!

'Martin. You'll get there quicker if you let us help!'

Stupid asthma. Stupid inhaler. Leave me alone!

They didn't. They made sure I was all right. Then they walked home with me.

'Thank you so much for bringing him back home,' gushed my mum. She does a lot of gushing. She has to. It's her job. She runs the Burlington Hotel, on the sea front.

'It's his asthma, you know.'

Go on mum, let everyone know. I don't know why she doesn't go the whole hog and use a loud hailer. That Brightly woman, a friend of hers who works on the local paper, was with her, grinning away like a chat show host.

'The doctors say it's the traffic you know, Sarah. We moved down from London to get away from it, but it's getting just as bad down here. Now there's something you could write about. Traffic fumes. That would make a change from headlines about Prize Leeks.'

'We have done stories about traffic pollution... But it's old hat now. The editor always wants *new* stories.'

The Brightly woman went off down the promenade and Nitro-Jen stared after her like she was some sort of heroine.

'That's Sarah Brightly from the *Gazette*, isn't it?'

'That's right,' said mum.

'Wow!' said Nitro-Jen.

She's easily impressed. She wants to be a journalist when she leaves school. I know. I heard her telling Miss James, our English teacher.

I shuffled up the steps to go inside. Mum tried to drag me back.

'Thank you again girls. Say good bye to your friends, Martin!'

'Bye, bye Martin!' called Ammonia. Her sarcastic voice again.

They wandered off. Ammonia no doubt keen to tell Nitro-jen how disgusting I was.

'They are not my friends!' I hissed.

Mum sighed one of her pathetic sighs. 'Yes, all right.'

We were making our way to the stairs to go up to the flat when Old Granny Grant slithered out of the lounge.

'Mrs Rowlands!'

Mum had one of her sudden bouts of deafness and headed straight for the stairs.

'Mrs Rowlands! Don't run away!'

But not quickly enough. Old Granny Grant got there first. She was brandishing a copy of the *Gazette*.

'Have you read this?'

MYSTERY ILLNESS WORSE! screamed the headline.

'Yes, Miss Grant, I know,' gushed mum.

'Twelve more people struck down by this dreadful

plague. Because plague is what it is. And they still don't know what's causing it. This town isn't safe!'

Mum had her excuse ready to hand. It was me.

'I'm sorry, but Martin isn't feeling well. It's his asthma. If I can just get him upstairs. Good evening Mrs MacDonald...'

By now Old Granny Grant's crony, Mrs Wimpy, had appeared, cooing and twittering away like a demented pigeon.

'Ooo, ooo...the poor, poor boy.'

'What are you "oo-ooing" at,' snapped Old Granny Grant to her friend. Mrs Wimpy looked down at her brown lace-up shoes, like a kid who has been told off by teacher.

Mum and I almost fell over each other in our attempts to get upstairs to the flat and away from the old biddies' clutches.

The flat is at the top of the hotel; right along the corridor from Old Granny Grant's and Mrs Wimpy's room.

During the day, I can stand at my window in my room and look down at the prom. I see people yakking away to each other. They don't see me. And

I don't hear what they're saying. It's like watching the telly with the sound off. Sometimes I make up stories about them and write them down in my diary.

Night time: that's when my room is the best place to be. During the night, I can look out of my window and see the universe. Mum got me the telescope when dad went. When I look up at the night sky through my telescope, nothing on Earth seems very big any more.

That evening, when I looked through my telescope, I saw a big yellow star. A perfectly shaped five-pointed star. It was clearer than any star I'd ever seen before. And no wonder. It was one of those sticky gold stars you get in the Infants' for doing something really clever like tying up your shoe lace or lasting a whole ten minutes without asking to go to the toilet. And it was stuck on the end of my telescope.

There was a knock at the door and Chef came in with a tray of grub. Leftovers from the evening meal downstairs.

'Food for the invalid.'

'I suppose this was you?'

'Ah, yes. My star. Did you think you'd found a new planet?'

Chef was laughing. Chef was always laughing.
But in a jolly, bubbly sort of way. He was the only
person I didn't have a nickname for. I didn't even
know what his real name was. We all just called him
Chef. Chef was all right. We were always playing
jokes on each other.

'Martin. Are you going to eat any of this?'

But I was too busy looking through the telescope. I
was checking to make sure that Chef's sticky star

hadn't left a mark on the lens. But I could see
something else. Something out there in the sky.

If I'd been looking through binoculars, I would
have said that it was a bird, hovering. It had wings;
white, curved, gracious wings. But these wings did
not flap like a bird's. They were fixed. And it glowed
with a warm glow, like hot coals in a fire.

'Chef! Quick! Look at this!'

I pulled Chef to the telescope.

'Have a look! Can you see it?'

Chef paused.

'Wow! Oh yeah! Amazing!'

'Let's have another look.'

But when I took the telescope back to have another look, the beautiful white object had gone.

'It's gone…!'

'Well, well, fancy that!'

'But you saw it Chef. You said you saw it!'

'What I saw, Martin Rowlands, was your little joke. Paying me back for the sticky star. OK. We're quits now.'

'No, it wasn't! I saw something!'

'What?'

I knew what I'd seen. And I knew what it was.

'A spaceship,' I said quietly.

Then mum came in.

'What's up now?'

'Martin's seen a spaceship,' said Chef.

'He's always seeing spaceships. Martin, just who fills your head with such nonsense I don't know, but you're probably suffering from lack of food.'

'I don't want leftovers!' I shouted. And ran all the way downstairs to the dining room.

Mrs Wimpy was there with Old Granny Grant.

'Feeling better dear?' she cooed.

Why does everyone seem to think I'm some sort of freak? I stood there trying to think of something rude to say to them; something rude enough to make me feel good, but not so rude it would get me into trouble.

But before I had time to think of something suitable the sky caught fire.

At least that's what it seemed like. There were sparks flying like giant fireworks and a magical white glow that lit up everywhere like daylight. Then there was a huge hiss and roar as if someone had dropped a giant hot frying pan into a tub of water. And it all went quiet for a second or two. Until a piercing shriek split the air. It came from under the table. It was Old Granny Grant. She'd taken cover and was hysterical.

'It's coming for me! It's coming for me!'

'It's all right,' soothed Chef. 'It's all right.'

'What was it?' shuddered Old Granny Grant.

'I don't know,' shrugged Chef.

'Then how do you know it's all right? You silly, silly man!' wailed Old Granny Grant. And she was off again.

Ten minutes later, the whole of Southbeach was ambling round outside the hotel. Ammonia and Nitro-Jen were there. They came charging up to mum, like she was an old friend of theirs. Huh! Just because they had brought me home.

'You must've had a direct view from the hotel,' Ammonia was saying.

'Yes,' said mum, 'what was it?'

But Ammonia didn't know. Nobody knew. Except me. But then nobody bothered to ask me. I could have told them it was a space craft and that I had seen it through my telescope.

The Brightly woman was buzzing about getting eye witness reports for the *Gazette*. The police were busy marking off part of the prom and the beach with tape. Completely the wrong place, of course. Nowhere near where I'd seen the space craft dropping down out of the sky. A driver got out of his car and started arguing with the police to let him through. It was Moneybags Belcher.

'Look at him. Mr High-and-Mighty Belcher. Thinks he owns the place,' muttered Ammonia.

'He does own the place,' replied mum. 'Most of it, any way.'

And if he had his way, he'd own a bit more of it –

the Burlington Hotel, I thought. Belcher has been trying to get mum to sell him the hotel for ages now. Not that she ever would, of course. She's not *that* stupid. The nicest thing you could call Belcher is a toad, but that would be unfair to toads.

'He tips stuff from his factory into the sea,' Ammonia went on. 'Disgusting.'

Nitro-Jen had turned beetroot. 'No he doesn't! They had an inquiry didn't they – and they didn't find any evidence at all. I should know. My dad works there!'

I left them arguing and wandered across nearer the police tape. Standing by Belcher's car was his daughter, Claire. She often comes into the hotel with him. She's dead posh. She used to be in the same class as me at the Infants', but now she goes to a fancy private school where they wear pink blazers. I suppose if I'd been the sort to swoon over girls – which I am definitely not, I would have said she was quite pretty really. She caught me looking at her.

I turned away and looked out to sea in the direction I had seen the space craft.

There was nothing. Nothing but the reflected lights of the sea front illuminations dancing up and down on the dark water.

2 Day one

It was amazing. The goings-on in Southbeach on Day One Minus One were all over the papers, even the *Daily News*. I don't think Southbeach had been in a proper newspaper since Queen Victoria was forced to stop off here when the royal train broke down in about eighteen hundred and something. All right, so the story *was* in the bottom corner of page seven. After all the stories about soap opera stars, the royals and all that lot. But at least we were in the proper newspapers. Not that it impressed Old Granny Grant.

'Phoo-ey!' she bellowed, over her All Bran. 'I've

been in electrical storms in the Pacific and whatever it was last night, it was no electrical storm.'

For once I had to agree with her.

I got down to the beach as soon as I could. There was no one around. This was hardly surprising. The average age of the population of Southbeach is about a hundred and ninety. Most of the old dears take half the morning just to get their false teeth in.

The tide was out. I walked to the edge of the water. I looked out to sea. I suppose I expected to see one of those inflatable life rafts that round-the-world yachtsmen have, but there was nothing. The sea pulled gently at my feet. I looked down and saw sand and pebbles washing over the toes of my trainers. Just to my left, I noticed the sea had left behind little pools, where something had made deep impressions in the sand. Then I realised just what these deep impressions were. Footprints.

I followed them back up the beach. There was just one set. About the size of a grown-up's, but not the right shape for either a bare foot or a shoe. Right in the middle of the beach, they stopped. So I followed them back to the water's edge and saw that they appeared further along the beach. I was running now, following the footprints away from the sea. The

faster I ran, the more excited – and the more scared –
I got. I prayed the asthma wouldn't come back. Just
as I got to the top of the beach, where the fisherman
haul up their boats, I heard a scream. I looked up. It
was Nitro-Jen. And Ammonia of course. Those two
were like fish and chips. You never got one without
the other.

'Are you two following me, or what?'

'Shhh…! Keep your voice down, megamouth,' hissed Ammonia, bossy as always.

'It wasn't me who screamed like a maniac.'

'You would've done, if you'd stumbled against this,' whispered Nitro-Jen. She beckoned me down. And I gulped, broke out in a sweat and tingled all the way up my spine. But I definitely did not scream. Crawling out from under a tarpaulin was a…*thing*. It was covered in a browney patterned shell, rather like a giant pine cone. It had arms and legs, was more or less human size and had the weirdest haircut I had ever seen.

'What is it?'

'I don't know, some sort of animal?'

'No! It looks human. Well…almost.'

'Jenny and I thought you might know where it came from…'

I knew all right. It came from a space craft that dropped like a bird from the night sky. But I wasn't going to tell them. At least, not yet. I shook my head.

'…Only we saw you having a nose out this way, last night. While all the kerfuffle was going on. You were making eyes at Claire Belcher.'

'I wasn't—' I protested.

'Sshh! It's moving!'

It very definitely *was* moving. We all stepped back. The thing slowly began to uncurl itself and I saw that on its right wrist was a huge band with dials and flashing numbers. Some sort of computer. The thing looked at it as if it was checking the time. Then it looked at us; a kind of squint, as if we were the ones that shouldn't have been there, not it. Then it spoke.

'Hy wung tai foo ho chi?'

'That's Martian, I expect,' said Ammonia.

'Sounds more like Chinese to me.'

'Do you speak Chinese then?'

'No. Do you speak Martian?'

The thing was thumping the computer gadget on its wrist, like it was trying to get it to work. Perhaps it had got water in it and it wasn't waterproof, I thought. The thing spoke again.

'Hello? Hello? Can you understand me?'

'That's English!' yelled Nitro-Jen.

She's *so* sharp.

'Ah, yes. Of course. English. I knew it was one of the silly ones. All these silly languages. Why all Earthlings can't just speak one language like every other planet I don't know.'

The thing got up and dusted itself down. It was pear-shaped. With arms and legs. I didn't like the look of it one bit.

'Where are you from? Mars?'

The thing shook with what seemed like anger. It was obviously very touchy. 'Do I look like a Martian?'

'I don't know. I don't know what people from Mars look like.'

'Where are you from then?' asked Ammonia.

'The planet Gia.'

'Never heard of it,' I snorted.

The thing shook again. 'Never heard of it? What are you?' it screamed at me, 'a nincomploop?'

'It isn't nincomploop, it's nincom*poop*,' explained Nitro-Jen.

'Down!' hissed Ammonia. 'Someone's coming!'

Old Granny Grant and Mrs Wimpy walked by; Old Granny Grant rabbitting on about how dreadful the hotel was and the mystery virus and something should be done about it...blah, blah.

'We'd better watch he isn't seen,' muttered Ammonia.

'I don't have to be seen if I don't want to,' replied

the thing. It stood there, sort of concentrating, for a moment. Then there was a plop, as if someone had uncorked a bottle of wine and the thing shrank and disappeared. There was another plop in the sand behind me and the thing reappeared.'Where did you learn to do that?' I think all three of us spoke at once.

The thing shrugged its scaly shoulders. 'In the Infants'. First Law of Abstract Matter.'

I let that one pass.

'So who are you? And what are you doing in Southbeach?' asked Ammonia.

'Call me Ollie,' said the thing.

'Ollie? That's a nice name,' said Nitro-Jen.

'It's not my name,' said Ollie, 'but you can call me that because it is a nice word. Ollie... Ollie... Ollie... I got it from an English song we learned at school. "The Ollie and The Hivey".'

And he suddenly started singing:

O-of all the trees that are in the wood
The Olly swears the clown.

One thing was obvious. Ollie was far better at disappearing than he was at English – or singing for that matter.

'You haven't any grub have you?' Ollie looked at Ammonia.

'I think he means he's hungry,' explained Nitro-Jen. I kept quiet. There was no way I was going to be yelled at by an alien again.

'I have been travelling for three weeks,' said Ollie, 'and I am starving.'

Ammonia fished out a packet of fruit gums. Ollie ate the lot in one noisy gulp, wrapper and all. Not even Roly Thompson eats sweet *wrappers,* and he could have hired himself out to the school dinner people as a human swill bin if he had wanted.

'But why did you come to Southbeach of all places?' asked Ammonia.

Good question, Ammonia, I thought. If I was an alien space traveller with amazing powers of disappearing, the last place I'd park my space craft would be Southbeach. EuroDisney perhaps, Alton Towers possibly, even the Australian outback, but Southbeach?

Ollie thrust back his shoulders, trying to make himself look important. 'I came here because Gia's Director of Inter-Planetary Research and Exploration ordered me here. I am on a mission. To save Southbeach.'

Save Southbeach from what, I thought. Being overrun by coachloads of holiday-making old age pensioners? But Ollie was going on.

'I shall need help. You three seem highly intelligent and mature people...

This alien with an exotic taste in haircuts did know what he was talking about, after all, I thought.

Jenny, Amina and I all smiled modestly and swaggered about a bit.

'...for Earthlings, that is,' continued Ollie. 'First of all, I shall need somewhere to hide.'

'I thought, being a "highly intelligent" Gian, you could disappear at will,' I replied sharply.

'That, like many other things, saps my energy.'

I wasn't impressed. 'So? I get tired too.'

'I'm not made of energy!' Ollie sounded like mum when I ask her for money for a school trip.

'The best place would be your mum's hotel, wouldn't it Martin?' suggested Amina. 'After all, there are plenty of spare rooms.'

We walked along the beach, shielding Ollie from the view of any passersby, until we came alongside the hotel. I thought, this is stupid, we should all be scared witless of this alien on his mission to save Southbeach, but we weren't. It was the way he lollopped along. It was that haircut. It made him seem *friendly* somehow. I wondered if he was scared of us.

'You stay here with Ollie. I'll go in and see if the coast is clear,' I said.

I swung myself up the promenade railings, and

gave Jenny, Amina and Ollie a wave as they tucked themselves away out of sight behind a breakwater.

When I turned to cross the sea front, I saw that parked on the double yellow lines in front of me was a big silver car: Belcher's. And as always, Claire Belcher sat in the front seat. And as always she was doing nothing; nothing but looking and watching. She gave me one of those half smiles which I pretended to ignore.

I only hoped she hadn't seen us on the beach. If there was an alien in town, Claire Belcher's old man would definitely want to buy it. And I wanted Ollie to be Jenny's, Amina's and my secret. For a bit at any rate. There were lots of things I wanted to know. About the stars and the planets and all that. Ollie might well know the answers.

I dodged behind Old Man Belcher's BMW and crossed the sea front to the hotel.

'Oi! You! Sonny Jim!'

I had hardly got both feet into the hotel, before this voice was yelling at me. It belonged to a bloke; tall, twitchy, dark. He looked as if he used cooking oil to keep his hair in place. He seemed to be a guest – but he was most definitely not an old age pensioner on holiday.

'Where can I get a cup of coffee in this so-called hotel?'

'The bar opens for coffee at eleven o'clock.'

Mum was always drumming it in to me to be smarmy – polite she called it – with guests. He wore one of those macs that have buckles everywhere. He jangled as he waved his fists in the air.

'Drat! I suppose I'll just have to take a walk out and see if I can find any signs of civilisation in this town.'

I tried to creep away, but he stopped me again.

'Hang on, hang on. Got another question for you.' He paused and leaned close. 'What do you know about this mystery illness?'

'It's just a bug I think.'

He didn't sound pleased.

'Or a virus. Nobody's sure really. And—'

'And what?'

And mum says it's ruining her hotel business I thought, not that I'd tell you. I shrugged my shoulders. 'That's all really. I think...'

'Real mine of information aren't you?' He smiled. One of those smiles that could have turned a pint of cream sour at a hundred metres.

'You staying here?'

'I live here.'

'Ah. The son and heir, eh? Well, if you hear anything, let me know. Joe Lowin's the name. *Daily News.*' And off he went. *Daily News* I thought. That'll put the Brightly woman's nose out of joint.

I could see mum in the office with old Moneybags Belcher. I slipped into the alcove under the stairs. Where the pay phone is. I could hear them from there, but not see them.

'…And that really is my final offer, Mrs Rowlands.'

'And I'm really not interested, Mr Belcher.'

'You can't go on forever, running a hotel with no guests.'

'*Two* guests. Or rather *three* now. We had a journalist from London book in this morning.'

'But it's the middle of the summer holidays, Mrs Rowlands. You should be full to overflowing.'

No reply from mum. Moneybags Belcher really knows how to twist the knife.

'They're still no nearer finding the cause of this mystery bug. Two more people went down with it yesterday.'

Still no reply from mum. This wasn't like her. Usually she gave Belcher as good as he got.

'Remember, Mrs Rowlands, *I* can afford to wait until things pick up. *You* can't.'

'Well, I'm not selling, Mr Belcher.'

She'd found her voice at last. Go on mum, tell him to push off!

But Belcher got in first.

'I don't suppose the bank is very happy, is it?'

'That is none of your business!'

Mum! Tell him, mum! Tell him to push off!

'What have they given you? Five days?'

'I'm not selling, Mr Belcher.' Mum's voice was almost a whisper.

'Are you sure, Mrs Rowlands...?'

'Yes...yes...I'm sure.'

I felt a little sick in my stomach as a panic seized me. For she didn't *sound* sure. Not to me. And if she didn't sound sure to me, she certainly wouldn't sound sure to Moneybags Belcher. I heard the front door swish. Belcher had gone. But he'd be back. Mum went scampering through to the kitchen. She didn't see me. Her eyes were all red. She would be going to give Chef a hand with the lunches. And with Old Granny Grant and Mrs Wimpy walking the prom, Joe Lowin out searching for civilisation, the coast was clear for the alien with the haircut.

I might have known it would start again. Just as I got back to the breakwater. All the air was in my chest and I couldn't get it out.

'What's he doing? Is there something wrong with him?' Ollie was saying, like I was a car that needed fixing. Stupid, stupid asthma. Nitro-Jen fussed around me with my inhaler. It was OK.

'You were ages!' Ammonia complained.

'Belcher,' I said. I was still a bit breathless. 'But he's gone now.'

'Does he want to buy your hotel?'

'How did you know, nosey?'

'Keep your hair on! I just guessed that's all. He wants to buy everything. My dad's says he's a vulture.'

'My mum won't sell our hotel to Belcher. Never. Ever. See?'

'All right.'

'Well, just you watch it, Sondhi.'

Then Ollie joined in: 'Temper, temper.'

I blew.

'You stay out of it, space melon!'

'Earthworm.'

I didn't care if this alien *did* know all the answers to my questions about the planets, I didn't care. What did it matter now, if mum was going to have to sell the hotel? Where would we go? Nothing mattered any more. I got up.

'Just stop it! Both of you!' Jenny yelled. 'Martin…where are you going?'

'To the police. I'm going to tell them there's a dangerous alien on the beach.'

No sooner had I said it, than I knew how stupid it sounded.

'Martin!' Ammonia's voice was urgent.

'What?'

'Do you think the police would believe you?'

She had a point.

'And even if they did, do you think they would believe Ollie?'

She had another point. That was the infuriating thing about Amina: her temper *was* almost as quick as mine and she *was* bossy – but she was usually right about things.

'OK Amina,' I said.

There was a sudden loud rumble. I looked up at the sky, thinking it might be thunder.

'That,' said Jenny with an air of disapproval, 'was *his* stomach.'

'I say, you haven't got any more grub, have you?' asked Ollie.

In the end it was decided that it would be safer to take him up to my room. I've got this ace creaking floorboard just outside my door. So I can always hear if anyone's on their way to my room. Which there usually isn't, apart from mum and Chef. I went down to the kitchen to see what I could scrounge in the way of food.

'Martin! You've hardly had time to digest your breakfast!' Mum's eyes were still red.

'Oh, let him have something,' said Chef. 'He's a growing lad, aren't you Martin?' He made me a cheese sandwich. 'Get that down you, and you'll soon have a splendid figure, like mine!'

This was not a happy thought. Chef was well on the way to becoming eligible for a Pavarotti look-a-like contest.

I sneaked a drink from the fridge. When I got back to my room, Ollie and the girls had really made themselves at home. Sitting on *my* bed looking at *my* computer.

'Scrummy!' said Ollie and wolfed the cheese sandwich down in one go.

'Scrummy?' I said, 'nobody says "scrummy".'

'Gians obviously do,' replied Amina. She *always* has to have an answer.

'Look at this, Martin!' Jenny was jumping up and down like a clown. 'Look what Ollie's got on the computer!'

'On *my* computer,' I muttered.

'It can interact with Ollie's wrist thing.'

'It has a compatible interface,' said Ollie. I hate computer whiz kids.

On the screen was some sort of map.

'It's a map of Southbeach,' chimed in Amina.

It didn't look like a map of Southbeach. It looked more like one of those weather maps you get on the telly, except there was a lot of red on it.

'The red's pollution,' explained Amina.

'About thirty-six and a half thousand Earth days ago,' began Ollie.

'Do you think he means a hundred years?'

'Shhh…!' Ollie said, as if he was the teacher and we were talking in class. I thought, this is *my* bedroom you're in.

'…the Director of Inter-Planetary Research and Exploration on the planet Gia sent out space probes to all known planets, including Earth. The Earth space probe landed around here.'

Jenny was quick off the mark as usual. 'And now you want it back?'

I put on one of my jokey voices. 'Excuse me mister, can we have our space probe back please?'

Jenny and Amina giggled, I can do really brilliant jokes. Ollie wasn't laughing. 'It's serious old chap. The signal that came through to the Director was Red Alert. An overload.'

'Overload?'

'Some sort of gunge and filth messing it up. That's why I've got to find it, before…'

'Before what?' asked Amina. Ollie had us all spellbound now.

'…before it blows. And if it blows, well, it's capable of a trillion and three megazyglots of Gian power.' He paused, as if he was doing a sum in his head. 'It could take the whole of Southbeach with it.'

'What!'

'Don't worry, we've got five days to find it.'

Ollie made five days sound like five centuries. He took a swig from his drink. Then suddenly dropped it, all over my new atlas.

'Hey, careful!'

'Sorry, old chap. I get clumsy. That's why I can't keep disappearing. It uses my energy and I get clumsy more quickly.'

Perhaps this alien works on batteries, I thought.

'But I should be all right for five days,' said Ollie,

confidently.

'And then what?'

'I'll be OK if I can get back to the space craft.' He swallowed hard. 'Otherwise I expire.'

Nobody said anything for a bit. Five days to save Southbeach says Ollie; five days to save the hotel says mum, I thought.

'You will help me find this space probe, won't you?' pleaded Ollie. Amina and Jenny nodded.

I poured the rest of his drink for him.

Ollie's wrist-computer thing had a device like a water diviner which would lead us directly to the space probe. It seemed easy enough. There was one major problem about taking Ollie with us on searches though and that problem was Ollie. Being a scaly, pear-shaped alien with a ridiculous haircut was going to attract attention – lots of it.

'We could pretend he's a human in fancy dress and we're collecting for Red Nose day,' I suggested.

'But it isn't Red Nose day,' retorted Amina. She always has to spoil a good idea.

'Why don't you stay here and give us the wrist-computer thing,' Jenny ventured.

Ollie snorted. 'Because you'd never manage to work it.'

'I would,' I replied. After all, it didn't look much different from a pocket calculator.

Ollie snorted again. 'Earthlings have only the most primitive understanding of microtechnology,' he sighed.

'Rubbish.'

'True!' protested Ollie. 'We learned it at school, in geography.'

Like I said, I *hate* computer whiz kids.

'A disguise,' said Jenny, 'that's what he needs.'

'Hey, you can't go in there!'

But she had. With a smart tug, she'd pulled open the door to my wardrobe and was nosing around inside. In no time, Amina had joined her.

'Oh look, Amina, he's got Edd the Duck pyjamas.'

'I don't wear those anymore, stupid!'

Then Jenny stopped squealing. 'Martin, I didn't know you were an Arsenal supporter,' she said. She was holding aloft my Arsenal scarf. The one dad had bought me.

'My dad's an Arsenal supporter,' she said.

'So was mine,' I said.

In the end we fitted Ollie up with one of my old blue sweatshirts, a pair of turquoise trousers, a jacket and a baseball cap. We made our way out of the side entrance, where it was quieter.

'What *does* he look like?' I asked, as Ollie waddled off down the road. Words like gormless, nit wit, brain dead sprang to mind.

'Seeing he's got your clothes on, he probably looks something like you,' said Amina. Her sense of humour was obviously very warped.

On the beach, Ollie tapped in a few figures on his wrist-computer thing. Then he shook it.

'Which way, Ollie?' Jenny was dancing from foot to foot, as if we only had five minutes to find the space probe, rather than five days.

Ollie hit his wrist-computer thing – hard. 'Er…we'll start looking here. Yes, why not?'

My mouth went all dry. Jenny stopped dancing about. Amina said, 'Ollie, I thought your wrist-computer thing could find the space probe.'

'Oh it could,' said Ollie, unhappily, 'once. But not now.'

'Why not?'

'It's been er…*clumsied*.'

'You mean broken?'

'It wasn't me!' Ollie seemed frightened and angry at the same time.

'I never said it was.'

'Look at it! Made in Jupiter. Cheap Jupiterian junk!'

'Can't you mend it?' asked Jenny wearily, as if she already knew the answer.

Ollie shook his head. 'No, not even this could mend it.'

From a small compartment on his wrist-computer thing, Ollie produced a ball, pearly white and shining.

'It's beautiful,' exclaimed Amina in a whisper. 'What is it?'

'This is what gives me my energy,' said Ollie.

'It may be beautiful, but it's not much use,' I said, bitterly, 'not if it can't mend your wrist-computer.'

'It *could*,' said Ollie, 'but it would leave me short of energy. I mean, what would be the point of knowing where the space probe was, if I hadn't got the energy to get to it and mend it? So like I said, we might as well start here.'

'Ollie, what does it look like, this space probe thing we're looking for?' Even at school, Amina was always the first one to put up her hand for questions.

'It's pink and it'll have little red lights and it's programmed to respond to the code name of

Charley.'

'What do you mean "programmed to respond to the code name of Charley?" '

'It's a voice-activated mechanism.'

'Oh I know, like you can get on telephones.' Trust Amina to know.

'Charley, Charley…' Ollie called, gently, as if he was singing to a baby, rather than trying to activate a computer-generated space probe.

There was no sign of Charley, though.

'The trouble is,' explained Ollie, 'you do need to get very close for it to respond.'

'And your way of getting close to it was your wrist-computer thing,' sighed Jenny.

'Which is now broken,' I added.

'How big is this space probe?' Amina asked.

'Oh, about this size.' Ollie picked up a rock. Then dropped it on his toe. 'Yee-ow!' he said. Hopping about on one leg, he ordered, 'spread out and comb the beach.'

'Ollie!' Jenny shook her head in exasperation, 'it'll be like looking for a needle in a haystack!'

'That's a rather quaint old English expression,' mused Ollie. 'You know, I've never heard it before.'

'And another "quaint old English expression" I don't expect you've ever heard before is the one about being a few sandwiches short of a picnic,' I said. 'What do you expect us to do? Inspect every rock on the beach?'

Ollie glared at me. 'Have you got a better idea?'

'Yes,' said Amina. If her idea was anything like mine it was very rude and concerned just what Ollie could do with his stupid space probe.

But Amina's idea wasn't like mine.

'Ollie, you said that the space probe had got gunged up with filth and stuff.'

'That's right...'

'Then why don't we start looking in the most disgusting, gunge-ridden part of the beach?'

'And where's that?' asked Ollie.

I knew just what Amina's answer would be and so did Jenny.

'Amina! You're not going to start on about Belcher's again! There's nothing wrong with his factory. Look what happened when the *Gazette* printed that story about Belcher tipping chemicals into the sea – they had to print a big apology the next week.'

'Only because Belcher threatened to sue them and they got the wind up. Belcher's got money and he's the sort who always gets what he wants.'

Belcher's conversation with mum came flooding back to my mind. I knew just what Amina meant. Moneybags Belcher's factory was as good a place as any to start.

'I agree with Amina,' I said.

'But no one's allowed in there without a pass! There are DANGER KEEP OUT notices all round!' Jenny was frightened. Really frightened.

'Look, I don't want to put you into any kind of danger,' said Ollie, quietly. We had almost forgotten about him. 'Just show me where this factory is. I'll make my own way there.' He got up. Then tripped. 'Oops. Clumsy me.'

'And then what will you do? Fall over? I'm coming with you,' said Amina.

'Me too,' I found myself saying, much against my better judgement.

Jenny smiled, weakly; then shrugged. 'Oh well, safety in numbers, I suppose,' she said.

Belcher's factory was quite a walk away at the far

end of the beach; way past all the hotels and
souvenir shops and bingo halls. Jenny and Amina
each took one of Ollie's arms to try and save some of
his energy. Walking along the beach, it was amazing
what we found. Drinks cans, plastic bottles, broken
glass, crisp packets.

'It's the non-biodegradable stuff that's the worst,'
said Ollie. For a Gian whose English was sometimes
very dodgy, he knew some very long words.

'The non-*what*?'

'All that plastic stuff.' Ollie was into his stride

now. 'Your natural Earth products such as wood or paper decompose, but plastics don't. So they're going to be cluttering up your planet for hundreds of years. Space scientists on Gia believe it could cause a massive earth warp.'

'A what?' I asked.

'So much junk and waste could tilt the earth's eco-system so that it becomes all lop-sided – an earth warp.'

Amina stooped down and picked up one of those clear plastic things that holds packs of drinks tins

together. 'I once saw a gull,' she said. 'It had got its head stuck through one of these and couldn't get it off. It had probably given up trying. It was just going around with it round its head and through its mouth. It couldn't eat. I threw it some bread. All these other gulls got there first. It made me feel sick. It wouldn't let me near it to get it off. I *would* have done. I tried…People don't *think*!'

We were all quiet for a minute. For the first time, I realised that Amina really did *care* about our planet Earth.

Ollie said quietly, 'I'm glad it was you three who found me yesterday.'

'Why?' I asked, fishing for compliments.

He looked straight at Amina. 'You really believe in *life*. In the life on your planet.'

'But it's all such a mess,' sighed Amina.

'You can do anything, if you believe in it enough,' said Ollie.

'Perhaps you can,' said Amina doubtfully. 'If you're a grown-up.'

'Huh! Grown-ups!' said Ollie. 'Who needs them!'

'Aren't you a grown-up then?' asked Amina.

'Me!' Ollie laughed. 'I'm half a thousand

xigatrons, which in Earth years is…' He fiddled with his wrist-computer thing. 'At least the calculator bit still works. Yes, in Earth years I have twelve and a half ears.'

'Eh? Ollie, your English—'

'It's better than *your* Gian.'

'You're trying to say that you're twelve and a half years old?'

'And why not? You've heard me speak of the Director of Inter-Planetary Research and Exploration?'

'Often.'

He did another calculation.

'She's fourteen.'

There wasn't a lot you could say to that.

The sea looked dark and cloudy, except for a large area next to Belcher's factory. Here the water was an electric green. Some sort of dead fish, wide-eyed and bloated was floating on top of the bubbling foam. Belcher's factory itself was surrounded by a wire fence. It was a cluster of dirty stone-grey buildings. There weren't many windows. There were even fewer doors.

'The probe must be around here somewhere,' declared Amina excitedly. 'Try calling it, Ollie.'

Ollie sang 'Ch-a-a-r-r-l-e-y!'

'Oi! You kids!'

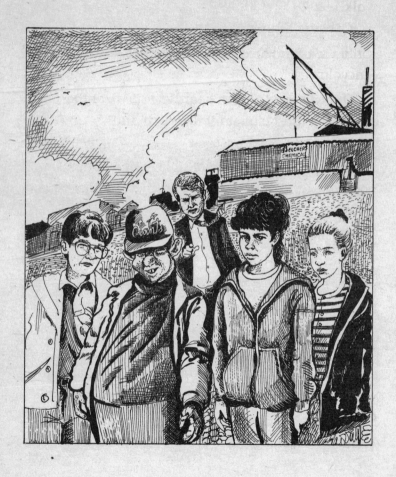

We spun round to face Moneybags Belcher.

'Lost something?' Belcher didn't know just how right he was.

'No,' said Amina calmly, 'we're just out for a walk.'

'I don't like kids around my factory,' Belcher continued. He looked hard at Ollie. 'Particularly kids in fancy dress. It's dangerous. So go on. Scarper – or else.'

'Or else what?' Steady on, Amina, I thought. I was ready to make a run for it.

Belcher didn't like her tone either, which was hardly surprising. He took out a portable phone from his pocket, you know the sort all posers use. 'Either you go away – or the police come and take you away.'

'We haven't done anything,' protested Jenny.

'That's what *you* say,' chortled Belcher, 'but who do think the police will believe? Me – or you?'

We didn't bother to give him an answer to his question, but made our way back along the beach towards the hotel.

I turned and looked back at the factory. Belcher was getting into his car. In the passenger seat sat Claire.

She was looking our way.

Ollie didn't say anything all the way back to the hotel. I think he was depressed. We were all depressed. We got Ollie up to my room and he curled up in the corner.

When we got back up to my room, we were not only depressed but angry. 'I'm going to make a call; report Belcher,' said Amina. 'Where's your pay phone?'

We left Ollie curled up in a corner and went downstairs. Joe Lowin, from the *Daily News* – Mr Smarm himself – was on the phone. He was not in a good mood.

'I don't know why you've sent me down here,' he was yelling down the phone. 'It's the middle of nowhere and there's nothing happening, nothing! A few old biddies laid up with the flu if you ask me. There's no mystery about it. So do you want me to come back? What else am I going to find?'

He slammed the phone down and stormed out. It was a good job we weren't in the way or we would've been trodden into the carpet.

Amina grabbed the phone.

'Who was that guy?' asked Jenny.

'His name's Joe Lowin.'

'And he's the Number One Reporter on Britain's

Brightest Daily!' Sarah Brightly from the *Gazette* appeared with mum. 'They must think this mystery illness scare is big news if they've sent him down here.'

Amina got through to the Water Board. 'I'd like to report some pollution. At Belcher's in Southbeach.'

Sarah shook her head. 'You'll be lucky,' she said to Jenny. 'Ken Belcher is too big even for the *Gazette* to take on. The trouble is, he always seems to know when he's going to be inspected. So he has time to clean up. Nobody's ever managed to get any real evidence. I don't expect Ken Belcher will be greatly troubled by the Water Board.'

Mum overheard this. You could tell by her face that she was thinking the same as I was. If Belcher was too big for the *Gazette* and the Water Board, then he was certainly too big for mum to take on. She mooched off to the office and I followed. 'Don't worry mum,' I said, 'I'll think of something.'

'I don't know what you're talking about, Martin, I really don't.' She did; I could see she did. She changed the subject. 'So those nice girls are your friends now, are they?' Amina and Jenny were beckoning me from the stairs.

'Well, sort of,' I said. And I dashed out.

We made our way back up to my room.

Amina was full of it. The Water Board were going to send an inspector down to Belcher's. I sighed. It was all very well for Amina to get on her high horse about Moneybags Belcher and to report him to the Water Board, but that didn't help Ollie to get his space probe back. Five days, Ollie had said and we'd already used up half a day. We would have to go back to Belcher's factory. There was no doubt about it.

'It's all right, Ollie, it's only us,' I called as we shuffled into my room.

I needn't have bothered. Ollie was nowhere to be seen.

Almost before we'd had time to stand and gawp, there was an angry shout from downstairs.

'Martin Rowlands!' Chef's voice. 'I want my cake back!'

'Ollie,' muttered Amina.

'Ollie,' echoed Jenny.

'Ollie,' I cursed, making his name sound like a swear word.

We charged back downstairs to the kitchen. Chef was fuming.

'Is this one of your little jokes, Martin Rowlands,

eh? I mean just what is going on?'

Well might he have asked. One of his precious
sponge cakes had been got at, as if someone had
taken a very blunt chisel to it. Suddenly, a piece of
cake began to move upwards off the plate, all by
itself. There was no doubt it was Ollie, making full
use of his powers.

'Er…Abracadabra!' declared Amina suddenly and she waved her arms about over the cake.

Chef's jaw dropped.

'It's a magic trick. How to get your cakes to rise. Er…and disappear,' she added, as the piece of cake vanished. We stood around looking sheepish, while Chef carried on fuming.

'I think he's gone,' I whispered to Amina.

'You think *who* has gone?' snapped Chef.

There was a piercing shriek from the upstairs landing. We dashed out. Joe Lowin was already on his way upstairs. Mum was following him, with Moneybags Belcher, of all people, in tow. He shot an ugly look over his shoulder at Amina as we dashed up the stairs behind him.

On the top landing Mrs Wimpy was crouched on the floor, fanning Old Granny Grant.

'It fell over. All by itself,' twittered the old dear.

A flower vase lay shattered at her feet. All the grown-ups looked at her as if she'd lost her marbles. Then, all of a sudden, it seemed to get lighter in the hall.

No wonder. My bedroom door was opening, all by itself, letting in the sunlight. Without a word, mum, Moneybags Belcher and Joe Lowin ran down the corridor to my room. And we followed. But no sooner had everyone got to my bedroom door, than Old Granny Grant screamed again.

Mum turned round sharply. 'What is it this time…'

Her voice trailed off. We could all see what it was this time. The vase, which had been shattered into tiny pieces a minute before, was now whole again.

'It's all right Miss Grant,' soothed mum. She looked accusingly at us.

'Er…Amina did it,' I said quickly.

'What!' Amina looked daggers at me. I headed back downstairs, Amina on my heels and everyone else in pursuit, sensing that we knew something.

'Yes, that's right,' Jenny was nodding her head. 'She does magic tricks.' Jenny spoke slowly and clearly to Amina, as if she was talking to a nit wit. 'Don't you Amina?'

Amina twigged. At last. 'Oh yes,' she said. 'That's right.'

'She wasn't even here,' protested Joe Lowin.

'That's how good she is,' I put in, quickly. 'She doesn't even have to be there.'

'Show us another one then,' said Belcher. I could tell he recognised us all.

'Er…I can't think of any more,' said Amina. She was getting just a little windy.

'Do that one with the vase again,' grunted Belcher.

'Yeah,' said Joe Lowin.

We were all in reception now. The grown-ups were all crowding Amina, so they didn't see the phone rise from the reception desk all by itself.

'Ollie!' muttered Amina. In a loud voice she said, 'I'll do another one. You see that phone behind you, on the desk?' The grown-ups all spun round. 'I can make it rise into the air, all by itself.'

And she did. Or rather, the invisible Ollie did.

Joe Lowin was impressed. 'Cor. She should be on television. Forget the boring mystery illness, this is a real front page story.'

And off he went.

Mum went back to the office, leaving us alone with Moneybags Belcher. He was blocking our way out. All of a sudden he grabbed Amina's arm. Hard.

'You,' he hissed in her ear, 'little Miss Magic. Don't try stirring it with the Water Board. My contact there told me about your call. Very silly. You didn't seriously think they'd send an inspector out to me? Good old Ken Belcher? You know what they call me in the business?'

Amina shook her head.

'Mr Clean!' said Moneybags Belcher triumphantly.

'It'll be different – one day!' said Amina defiantly.

'Oh no it won't,' laughed Belcher. 'Do you kids really believe you can change anything?' I remembered Ollie's words, *you can do anything if you believe in it enough.*

Belcher let go of Amina and turned to us all. 'Stay away from my factory. All of you.'

After he had gone we all looked at each other.

'You all right Amina?' I asked.

She nodded. But I could see she was dead upset.

'He was *really* angry you know,' Jenny said.

Amina said, 'Yes and that can mean only one thing. He's got something to hide.'

'Yes,' I agreed, 'Ollie's space probe for a start.'

The others looked glum.

'Don't worry,' I said. 'We've still got four whole days to find it.'

It was meant to be a sort of joke. But it came out really sarcastic.

My jokes always do that when I'm worried.

3 Day two

DAILY NEWS

MORE DETAILS.... EVENT

Pg. 2

INCREDIBLE MYSTIFYING MAGIC!

NIMINA SONDI FROM SOUTH BEACH, IS ALREADY A MASTER MAGICIAN AND SHE IS ONLY TWELVE

'The name's *Amina*, actually,' muttered Amina. She was really embarrassed about the article, probably because it was only on page two and not on page *one*. She was also angry with Ollie. We all were.

'Why did you fool about with all those tricks?' asked Jenny, rather more gently.

Ollie just shrugged, like he was sulking.

'It got us into trouble,' I added.

'It must have used up tons of energy from your

magic sphere thing,' fumed Amina.

I'd not thought of that.

'What's the point?' grumbled Ollie. 'We'll never find the space probe. Not with a clumsied computer. Not when we can't get near that factory place. So I decided to have a bit of fun. Nothing wrong with a bit of fun, is there?'

'Ollie,' said Amina severely, 'grow up. We've got four days left. Now come on.'

'You know,' said Ollie, 'when you talk in a bossy way like that, you sound just like the Director of Inter-Planetary Research and Exploration.' He sighed. 'OK, you chaps, you win. What's the plan?'

'We're going back to Belcher's this afternoon,' said Amina. 'And remember, Ollie, no tricks.'

Ollie tripped up half a dozen times on the way to Belcher's. Amina, Jenny and I took it in turns to support him. He seemed really heavy.

This time there was no sign of Belcher's car and we walked up towards the gates. A guy was wheeling some big canisters about.

'It's dad!' said Jenny.

He came over. He didn't look too happy at seeing

us. Ollie hung back and pulled my cap down over his eyes.

'What do you think you doing, hanging around here, Jen?'

'We're just out for a walk, dad.'

'Well, walk somewhere else.'

'What's wrong with around here?' asked Amina.

'It's a factory, not a beauty spot. And besides, if Belcher catches you, there'll be trouble for all of us.'

'Right. We'll leave it – for now,' said Amina. You could tell she meant – *and we'll come back when you've gone home.*

'Just…leave it,' said Jenny's dad, sternly.

Back home we went.

'We'll give if one more go tomorrow,' said Amina. 'And if your dad sends us away again, then we'll have to try a night visit.'

'I don't want to come,' said Jenny. 'You heard what my dad said. If Belcher catches us – me – again, it'll mean trouble. My dad would lose his job.'

'I don't know how he can bear to work there anyway,' said Amina.

'He has to work somewhere!' Jenny was almost in tears.

'What? Poisoning the sea? You heard what Ollie said…all the waste and rubbish could cause a massive earth warp!'

'There aren't that many jobs in Southbeach!'

I thought I ought to stop them arguing, but I didn't know how. I didn't know who was right. Perhaps they both were. Then Jenny turned and ran off up the road.

Ollie and I stood on the back doorstep. He was leaning heavily on my arm.

Amina said to me, 'I take it you're not backing out, too?'

'No. No…' I stuttered.

'Good. See you tomorrow,' she replied.

I nodded. I wasn't looking forward to it one bit.

Later, getting on for bedtime, Ollie and I were looking at the pollution map on the computer screen when the floorboard creaked. Ollie disappeared.

It was mum. She sat down on the bed and tried to make conversation about my telescope and the pollution map and Amina's tricks. I couldn't stand the suspense any longer.

'What is it mum?'

She took a really deep breath. 'Martin. I have a problem. A serious problem.

The hotel's losing money, I thought.

'The hotel's losing money,' she said. 'No one wants to come to Southbeach for their holidays while there's a mystery illness about.'

We owe the bank a lot of money, I thought.

'We owe the bank a lot of money.'

We've got to sell to Moneybags Belcher, I thought.

'You've got sell to Mr Belcher,' I said.

'I've got to sell — You knew?'

'I guessed,' I said.

Mum went on quickly. 'He's promised we can stay here of course and run the place. And the staff can stay on—'

'But even if he keeps his promise, the place will be *his*.'

'Yes, Martin, I know. And I haven't given him my final answer yet. I saw the bank yesterday. And they gave me—'

'Five days.'

'How did you know?'

I couldn't tell her I'd been listening in at the office door. Five days. Once it would have seemed an age; a whole school week for goodness sake. But now, it seemed like not enough time for anything.

'Anyway,' mum was saying, 'I thought I ought to tell you. I'm sorry.'

When she had gone, Ollie appeared again and curled up on my bed. I told him everything.

'Martin...'

'What?'

'Sorry your mum's got to sell your place. To that awful Mr Burper.'

'Yeah.'

I got dad's Arsenal scarf out of the wardrobe and put it under my pillow. It helps me find answers sometimes.

'What are you doing?' asked Ollie.

I told him.

'Have you got a spare?' asked Ollie.

'No,' I said, 'but you can wear my Arsenal hat if you like.'

He put it on.

'Come on you Gunners!' I said. And then wished I hadn't, because I had to explain to Ollie what it meant. 'It's like…you're willing them on to get on with it…to score a goal…to win,' I said.

'Gone on you Comers!' said Ollie, sleepily.

'Night Ollie.'

'Night Martin.'

It felt like my head had only just touched the pillow when there was another almighty scream from down the corridor. I opened my eyes. Light was streaming in the room. The door was open. Ollie had gone walkies.

Out in the corridor, once again, Old Granny Grant was being comforted by Mrs Wimpy. Joe Lowin was there, of course. But this time he was really excited. With a sinking feeling in my stomach I knew why, even before he started yelling at everyone in sight.

'Cor! I've seen it! I've seen it! A monster! An alien! A mutant martial arts wotsit space monster alien ET creature from another planet!' They weren't exactly the words I would have chosen at that precise moment to describe Ollie, but then I wasn't an ace reporter. Stupid Gian melon would have been *my* choice.

Joe Lowin was stumbling downstairs. 'An alien – in an Arsenal bobble hat! They'll have to hold the front page when I tell them about this. They'll just have to!'

And they did.

4 Day three

In the kitchen you could have sliced the air with a
Stanley knife. Chef was muttering to himself under
his breath. Mum kept shooting me dirty looks; she
was sure it was all something to do with me, but she
couldn't work out how. Even when I offered to help
with the guests' breakfasts she took it as a sign that I
must be feeling guilty about something. Which I
was. But I had left the 'something' I was feeling
guilty about in my bedroom and I had locked the
door.

The only one who seemed to be enjoying it all,
apart from Joe Lowin, was Mrs Wimpy. She was

shovelling her porridge down like a navvy filling a cement mixer.

'Ooh, wasn't it exciting last night!' she clucked.

Old Granny Grant obviously disagreed. 'I shan't be able to sleep another night in this place,' she grumbled, calling mum over. 'Mrs Rowlands, I would be grateful if you would prepare our bill for us. I have decided we're going. Immediately after breakfast.'

Mrs Wimpy looked up from her porridge. 'No! I'm staying here. If you feel like going Edith, then go you must.'

Old Granny Grant looked as if she couldn't believe her ears. We *all* looked as if we couldn't believe our ears. Mrs Wimpy never said boo to a goose, let alone no to Old Granny Grant.

'Well Enid...' she muttered. 'That is to say...I wouldn't want to leave *you*.'

'Oh don't worry about me,' smiled Mrs Wimpy. 'I shall be perfectly all right on my own. You know, nothing quite like this has ever happened to me. Do you think we shall be on the television?'

Old Granny Grant huffed and puffed some more. Then she said, 'Mrs Rowlands, forget what I said about leaving.'

Mum oozed charm. 'Of course Miss Grant.'

But Old Granny Grant hadn't quite finished. 'Perhaps you would be so good as to keep your space creature whatever-it-is in its quarters at night.'

'Oh, don't be such a scaredy cat,' laughed Mrs Wimpy. Old Granny Grant turned beetroot.

Seeing Ollie certainly seemed to have done Mrs Wimpy some good. It was almost as if she had acquired some of Ollie's energy.

He was still sleeping when I got back to my room. He

managed to wolf down the two pieces of toast I had smuggled out of the kitchen for him though.

'I'm not even going to risk going downstairs with you,' I told him sharply. 'Joe Lowin's got the place crawling with press photographers all wanting a picture exclusive of you. This time it's out through the fire escape.'

He was still sulking when we climbed through the fire escape door onto the top of the ladder.

'I don't like this.'

'Tough.'

'I don't like heights!'

'Ollie. You've been in a space craft! Up into the stratosphere and beyond.'

'I know, but I wasn't looking then.'

I took his hand and we went down one step at a time. I left him quaking on the bottom flight of the fire escape while I went to look for Amina. I found her lurking round the front with Jenny. I beckoned them round the corner.

They had read all about the MUTANT SPACE MONSTER MAYHEM, of course.

'Why did you do it Ollie?' asked Jenny.

He was still crouching at the bottom of the fire escape.

'I can't help it if I sleep walk,' he mumbled, pouting.

'He was going to nick more food from the kitchen,' I said. 'And anyway, what are you doing here, Jenny Steel, I thought you said yesterday you weren't coming on this expedition.'

Jenny looked glum. 'That's what I said. I didn't want to get my dad into trouble with Mr Belcher. But it's a bit late for that now.'

'What do you mean?'

'My dad's not working there any more after today.'

'You mean Belcher has sacked him?'

'No, he's going to quit. He's going in this morning to tell Mr Belcher and to get his things.'

'Why is he leaving?'

Jenny shrugged. 'I don't know. He wouldn't say.'

'I bet it's something to do with the pollution,' said Amina. 'I think Jenny's dad should get a medal for saying no to Belcher.'

I wished I could think of a way to get hold of enough money to help mum pay off the bank, so that *she* could say no to Moneybags Belcher, too.

'I've brought an empty bottle,' said Amina. 'I'm going to take a sample of the sea water. Then we can get it analysed.'

'How will that help us find the space probe?'

'It won't, but if the muck from Belcher's is damaging the space probe, think what it might be doing to Southbeach and the sea.'

'If only we can get close enough this time, Ollie can call the code name, can't you, Ollie? Ollie?'

We had been so full of our own ideas that we had forgotten about Ollie. He was way back, slumped against a breakwater. We ran back to him.

'He's getting more and more tired,' said Jenny.

'If the stupid melon hadn't spent most of yesterday smashing vases and "having fun" he might have a bit more energy left to look for his Charley thing and save Southbeach,' I said crossly.

'Why do you always have to go on at him?' Jenny looked at me as if I was some sort of bully.

'I don't! But you don't have to live with him, do you? Always whining for food, scaring old ladies – and he snores!'

'You're pathetic Martin Rowlands.'

'Come on you Gunners!' said Ollie suddenly.

Jenny frowned. 'What does he mean?' she asked.

'He means let's get on with it, shall we,' I said.

We got on with it. We half-carried, half-dragged
Ollie as far as the beach by Belcher's factory, where
he felt like another rest, so Amina went down to the
water's edge and got her sample. She put her arm in
right up to her elbow, 'so I get what's underneath
and not just the stuff on top,' she explained. 'It looks
disgusting, doesn't it?'

I was keeping look out and saw Belcher's car
arriving.

'Down!' I yelled, and we flung ourselves down
behind a breakwater. I stuck my head up over the
top for a peep.

'He's gone in. But Claire's in the car.'

'She always is,' said Jenny.

'I feel rather sorry for her,' said Amina. She smiled, wickedly, 'and so does Martin, I think.'

I couldn't stop the anger. 'Sorry for her? How could I feel sorry for *her*? When her stupid father comes in throwing his weight about and upsetting my mum and now he's forced her to sell and it's going to be his place—'

I hadn't meant all of that to come out. I hadn't meant any of it to come out. Amina said quietly, 'I thought you said your mum would never sell your hotel to someone like Belcher?'

'She won't,' I said defiantly. 'Because she'll get the money somehow. I know she will.' I wished I could believe myself.

'Come on,' said Jenny, 'I'm sure Claire Belcher isn't going to say anything about us to her dad. Let's see if we can get just a bit closer, then Ollie can try to call Charley.'

'Yes please,' said Ollie.

We all stood up. Then Amina sat down again.

'I– I don't think I feel very well,' she said. And she flopped right over, like a puppet when you let go of the strings.

'Amina!' yelled Jenny.

I looked around stupidly, as if a doctor or a grown-up was going to rise up out of the sea to help us. Then I turned to Ollie.

'Come on, you Gian genius! *You* must be able to do something!'

Ollie opened his mouth to speak, then saw something out of the corner of his eye. I followed his gaze. Haring down the beach towards us was Claire Belcher.

'Is she all right?' she asked.

'Does she look all right?' I replied.

All the time Jenny was trying to get Amina to come round.

'Claire!'

There stood Moneybags Belcher, red-faced and furious.

'Claire! Come back to the car! And you lot – scarper!'

'How can she scarper?' Jenny screamed at him, close to tears. 'She's ill!' Then a look of sudden relief came over her face. She was looking up the beach. We followed her gaze.

'Dad!' she yelled. 'Dad!'

Jenny's dad had just left his car at an untidy angle by the factory gate, its driver's door open. He must have been on his way to give in his notice to Belcher.

'Hey you!' called Belcher to Jenny's dad, 'you should be at work!'

But Jenny's dad ignored him and went straight to Amina. 'It's OK, Jen, I'll manage now.' He picked Amina up and carried her up the beach.

'You!' bellowed Belcher. 'You're fired! Do you hear me?'

'Too late, Mr Belcher,' said Jenny's dad. 'I quit.'

'Find Ollie,' Jenny hissed to me.

Ollie. Where was Ollie? I looked back down the beach. There was no sign of Ollie.

Claire was still there.

And I saw it all.

She was turned away from her dad and she had Amina's bottle in her hand. She looked as if she was going to throw it out to sea. I thought that's typical, she'll chuck it away to save her dad from getting into trouble and we'll never get to know about the poison in the river. But then she drew her arm back and stood there looking at the bottle and...*thinking*, I suppose. She took the top off the bottle, sniffed it, put the top back on and shoved it into her pocket. I watched her face. She was frowning, worried. She wiped her mouth with the back of her hand.

'What do you think you are playing at?' Belcher yelled at her. 'I told you to stay in the car! Never, but never go onto that beach!'

As Claire turned round to face her dad, she caught my eye. She looked troubled, sad. Her dad was still yelling at her.

Jenny's dad laid Amina in the back seat of his estate. Jenny got in with her.

'Jump in the front then, lad,' said Jenny's dad to me.

'Where is he?' hissed Jenny.

'Disappeared as usual,' I hissed back.

At the hospital, Amina was quickly surrounded by crowds of white coats. She looked like a science experiment. Then, pretty quickly, they sent us away. Jenny's dad dropped me off at the hotel. They were going round to tell Amina's mum and dad what had happened.

I heard his snoring before I had even reached my bedroom door.

'Ollie!'

He woke as soon as I came in the room. He looked perfectly at home in my bed.

'Hello old chap. How's Amina?'

'I don't know,' I sighed. 'Not very well,' I said. 'Did you manage to call up your Charley thing?'

Ollie shook his head. 'I need to get closer. And I couldn't. Not without your help, old chap.'

'Ollie?'

'Martin?'

'Your *English*.'

'I know, old chap. It isn't perfected. But it is—'

'Better than my Gian. I know. No, it's just…some of your words. "Old chap", "grub", "scrummy".'

'Ah. They are the sort of things only a nincomploop would say?'

'They're the sort of things that haven't been said by nincomploops or anybody else for about a hundred years!'

'Ah. I'm not surprised. We have very old learning modules on Gia. Taken from very old English books.'

'You're telling me.'

'And we have a very, very old English teacher. It's the cutbacks, you see.'

'Oh. Ollie?'

'Martin?'

'If…*when* we've found the probe and you've sorted it out. After…how will you get back to your space craft?'

'I'll just whistle it up.'

'Just whistle it up? You make it sound like a dog.'

Ollie began whistling, quietly; a strange haunting little tune, that seemed somehow familiar, but I didn't know from where; perhaps from way back when I was little. It was a tune that sort of swam in your head and drifted, drifted.

When I woke up it was…

5 Day four

It was hidden on page eighteen. I didn't have time to read on. I had to get to the hospital to see Amina.

I was swinging round the banister on the way up to my room, when my shoulder was jerked roughly from behind and I was spun round hard.

I found myself staring up into Joe Lowin's ugly face.

'Right, sonny Jim. What do you know?'

'What do you mean? What do I know about what?'

'The mutant alien monster thingie! I've promised my editor an exclusive – with photos – I want that story and I think you know something about it.'

I looked past Joe Lowin towards the hotel lobby. 'Hello mum!' I called.

She was nowhere in sight, of course, but Joe Lowin automatically spun round and let go of me. By the time he realised I had been calling to the parlour palm in the corner, I was off up the stairs. It seemed that I needed to use the fire escape for my entrances and exits now, as well as Ollie.

Ollie didn't think he'd make the walk to the hospital, so I put him on my bike. I ran behind, keeping hold of the saddle, until we got to the hospital. Then I thought it was safe to let go.

It wasn't.

'Ollie! Slow down! Use the brake!'

There was nothing wrong with the energy in Ollie's hands. Unfortunately. He yanked hard at the brake lever, locking the wheels. He flew over the handlebars and landed, haircut first, in the bushes.

He wasn't damaged and neither, thank goodness, was my bike.

We wandered into the hospital. I noticed a couple of nurses looking at Ollie.

'It's er…Red Nose day,' I explained. They didn't looked convinced. It was then I realised just how ridiculous Ollie looked. I had got used to him. I had even got used to the haircut, but one thing was certain, he wasn't going to get far in Southbeach Hospital without being stopped. He needed a disguise.

Two doctors came out of the room I had seen the nurses come out of. It was the obvious solution.

'Ollie! In there! Quick! And don't argue!'

He came out kitted up in all the proper surgeon's gear, including a face mask. I made him pull it right up to his eyes. Now he just looked like another doctor. Correction. Now he just looked like another doctor with a weight problem. We made our way towards the children's ward.

'Doctor! Doctor!'

It took a little while before I realised, with a lumpy feeling in my stomach, that the nurse hurrying towards us waving an x-ray wanted 'Doctor' Ollie's earnest medical opinion.

'Ah yes,' said Ollie, nodding his head at the x-ray. He paused, as if he was faced with a very difficult medical problem. 'Er...what is it?'

It was an x-ray of a hand. Even I could see that. And I could also see that the nurse was becoming very suspicious. I slipped behind her and held up my hand. To my relief, Ollie saw it.

'Ah yes. Five,' he said. I could see him mentally counting my fingers. In desperation I pointed to my hand.

'Er...what I mean is, five *point* five.'

'Come along doctor, please!' I yelled. And leaving the nurse standing there gawping like a goldfish, we ran for it.

I never feel very comfortable in hospitals. All the doctors and nurses look so important, rushing around saving lives. I always feel in the way. But the children's ward was better. Here were kids sitting up in bed eating burgers, watching cartoons on the telly – and it was noisy. But there was no sign of Amina.

'I'll do the talking, Ollie,' I said, shoving him out of the way behind one of those curtains on wheels that they pull round your bed. I found a nurse playing Scrabble with a boy who had his leg in plaster. 'Excuse me, I'm looking for my friend. She came in here yesterday.'

'The little girl who was knocked off her bike?'

'No, no...she er...' I wasn't quite sure how to describe Amina's 'mystery' illness. 'She was taken ill on the beach.'

The nurse stiffened and her face became serious. 'Oh dear, yes. She's in a side room on her own. Just round the corner.'

Ollie came out from behind the curtain and followed me at a distance. Nobody took the slightest notice of him.

The door to the side room was open and I walked right in.

'Hi Amina—' I stopped in my tracks. It wasn't

93

Amina.

'Hello Martin,' said Claire Belcher in a weak voice.

I didn't know what to say. 'Did you become ill on the beach as well?' I stammered.

Claire nodded. And then I remembered seeing her with Amina's bottle of sea water and how she had wiped her mouth with the back of her hand.

'I saw you. With Amina's bottle!'

'I know.' She seemed to find it difficult to talk, as if all she really wanted to do was to be asleep.

'What did you do with it?' I must have sounded really accusing.

'I gave it to the nurse.'

'And what's she done with it?'

'She took it to the laboratory.'

'Does your dad know?'

Claire shook her head. I tried to imagine what it must be like to tell on your dad. I tried to imagine what it must be like to have a dad like Belcher; how *bad* it must make you feel. Perhaps it was almost as bad as not having one at all.

Claire was looking at Ollie, who was eyeing a bowl of fruit on Claire's bedside cabinet, his surgeon's mask hanging around his neck. 'Why is your friend dressed up like a doctor?'

I gulped. Of course, she recognised him from the beach.

'Out!'

I spun round to see Moneybags Belcher's bulky frame filling the doorway.

'Don't you ever come pestering my little girl again!'

'Dad!' began Claire weakly, but no sooner had I retreated to the corridor than Belcher had seized Ollie by the shoulder. I saw with relief that he'd just had time to pull up his mask.

'Doctor!' pleaded Belcher, 'make her well again. Please. It's all I want.'

'I'll do my best,' muttered Ollie from behind his mask and marched out into the corridor.

When we found Amina, she looked as washed out and as listless as Claire. She managed to say hello before drifting off to sleep.

'Claire Belcher's got it too,' I said. Jenny snapped my head off.

'You went and saw Claire Belcher? How could you! It's her dad that's done all this!' She nodded in Amina's direction.

'It may be her dad that's done it,' I answered angrily, 'but it's not her!'

'Amina was right. You fancy her.'

'Oh shut up, Steel. You're so *childish*.'

'Shut up yourself.'

'Shut up both of you!' roared Ollie, so loud I thought it would bring the nurses running. 'The time for wars and arguments is long, long past,' he said. And you could see he meant it. He looked quieter, more serious, older somehow than I had ever seen him before. 'Today is day four,' he said. 'Tomorrow is the last day.'

Our racket had woken Amina. 'I'm sorry,' she said. 'We should be out there, looking.'

'Exactly. And you're not any use to anyone, lying here in a hospital.'

Ollie took the small pearl-white sphere from his wrist-computer.

'You can cure her with that?' I gasped.

Ollie shrugged. 'I can but try.'

Amina struggled to sit up. 'No!'

The illness is making her delirious or something, I thought.

'No!' Amina said again, firmly. 'Don't be stupid! How much energy will it take?'

'Quite a bit,' said Ollie quietly.

'Then you'll become weaker, perhaps even too weak to find the space probe with us – let alone get back to your space craft.'

'That's my problem,' said Ollie. He shook his head. 'You were right. I shouldn't have wasted all that energy on smashing pots and raising cakes. Anyway you can't stop me.'

Suddenly, the pearl-white ball began to glow, fiercely. Amina seemed to glow too. Then just as suddenly, the glow disappeared.

But Amina stayed sitting up. Her eyes were bright again.

'Well…?' asked Ollie.

'She certainly looks it,' I grinned. 'Well – *well*! Get it?'

Everyone groaned, then smiled. Like I said, I'm *brilliant* at jokes.

Amina, of course, wanted to get out of the hospital straight away and resume our search for Charley. The nurses, though, insisted that she stay in hospital for the rest of the day just in case she had a relapse. It was no good us even trying to explain that if you've had a powerful dose of cosmic life-force from the planet Gia you don't get a relapse.

Amina's mum and dad turned up, and as Jenny, Ollie and I made our way down the corridor, a familiar cry boomed out behind us.

'Doctor! Doctor!' It was Moneybags Belcher. He didn't seem to see Jenny and me, all he wanted was Ollie. 'She got better. My little girl got better!'

'Good,' replied Ollie, declining to shake Belcher's hand. Which was probably just as well; having your hand shaken by Ollie was like being squeezed by a cold kipper.

'You never cured that Claire Belcher as well?' asked Jenny.

'Of course I did,' said Ollie. 'Now take me home please Martin. I need to rest.'

We got Ollie out of his surgeon's gown and I took it back to the staff room. Then I put Ollie on my bike and the three of us set off towards town.

'We'll make a start on the search early in the morning,' said Ollie.

'It'll be day five already,' said Jenny.

'Just get me close enough to Charley so that it can pick up my voice-activated signal,' said Ollie, weakly. 'Don't worry. I'm sure I'll feel stronger by the morning.' He didn't sound too confident about it.

'I'll be getting home,' said Jenny.

'Got some writing up to do?' asked Ollie.

Jenny nodded.

'What writing up's that?' I asked.

Jenny blushed. 'Oh, nothing.'

'She's keeping a diary of everything that has happened to us over the last four days,' said Ollie. 'Then she's going to help Sarah Brightly write it all up for the *Gazette*.'

'Ollie!' hissed Jenny. She gave Ollie a really filthy

look. 'It was meant to be a secret!' She looked at me. 'I don't what you're laughing at Martin Rowlands.'

'Probably because *he's* keeping a diary, too,' chuckled Ollie.

'Ollie!' Now it was my turn to give him a filthy look.

Aliens can be *really* embarrassing at times.

I kept out of everyone's way. Joe Lowin and his photographer were still playing hunt the mutant space alien monster wotsit. In the kitchen, Chef was giving me funny looks. He had taken to locking his cakes up. And mum…Mum was walking round like a zombie.

Ollie slept all afternoon and all evening on my bed. I lay on the floor desperately trying to think of a plan to get mum some money so that we could keep the hotel. The more I thought about it, the more I doubted that Moneybags Belcher would let mum and me or Chef for that matter stay on once he owned the place. He just wasn't that sort.

I went to sleep knowing one thing. After tomorrow, whatever happened, nothing was ever going to be quite the same again.

6 Day Five

HERE IS THE NEWS AT EIGHT O'CLOCK ON WEDNESDAY 25 AUGUST. AMINA SONDHI 12, OF BEECH AVENUE SOUTHBEACH, AND CLAIRE BELCHER, 12, OF THE DRIVE, SOUTH BEACH, ARE BOTH AT HOME AFTER SHAKING OFF THE MYSTERY BUG IN SOUTH BEACH HOSPITAL YESTERDAY

The thing that went wrong first of all wasn't anything to do with the hotel and Moneybags Belcher or anything to do with the space probe blowing up. It *was* to do with Ollie though. We were waiting for the girls to arrive. Ollie was crashing around my bedroom like a clockwork toy that was out of control. Healing Amina and Claire had left him really clumsy. He was nervous and tense. And so was I. I kept telling him to sit down, but he wouldn't.

Then he crashed into my telescope.

I saw it wobble and topple as if in slow motion. It hit the corner of my wardrobe before crashing to the floor with a heavy thud. I scrambled across the room and picked it up. It rattled. When I looked through it, I couldn't see a thing. I choked back the tears.

'Ollie! My telescope!'

'Sorry old chap.'

'Sorry? Is that it? You've broken my telescope!'

'Sorry.'

'Mum bought me that. When dad went.' My most precious thing, destroyed. 'You stupid, ignorant, worthless space melon! You ought to be chained up!'

'I didn't mean—' stammered Ollie.

'Shut up!' I screamed.

Ollie curled up in the corner.

'Stay there! And don't you dare move!'

I stormed out of the room and locked the door behind me. I was going to ring Amina to find out where they had got to.

When I went into the office, I saw that mum had just put the phone down.

'Mum can I make a call?' I began. But she raced right past me, out into the hall and through to the kitchen. I ran after her. I stood by the kitchen door and listened.

'Chef. That was the bank,' she said. 'They won't change their minds. The five days are up. Unless I can show them a fuller order book by close of business this afternoon, they'll call in the receivers.' I heard her blow her nose. 'I'm bankrupt.'

'So you'll be selling to Belcher?'

'There's no other way. He says we can all stay on here.'

'And you believe him?'

'Of course I don't.'

Chef sighed, loudly. 'I can always get another job, but what will you and Martin do?'

'I don't know,' said mum quietly. 'I don't know.'

The desk bell in the hall suddenly rang, making me jump. I jumped out of sight into the alcove by the pay phone as mum hurried out of the kitchen to answer it.

'Good morning, Mr Belcher,' I heard her say. And then the office door slammed shut behind them.

I rushed out of the hotel and across the sea front. I felt I just had to get out of the hotel. Get some air. Anything. I leaned on the promenade railings and looked across the sand at the waves trickling up the beach. Out of the corner of my eye I could see Belcher's BMW parked outside the hotel. Out of the corner of my other eye I could see his filthy, poisonous factory. Everywhere I looked was Belcher, Belcher, Belcher.

Behind me a voice said, 'Penny for 'em, sonny.' It was Mr Smarm himself. Joe Lowin. His oily hair glistened. His face still had that twisted look, as if he was trying to learn to smile, but hadn't quite succeeded.

I tried to make my way back to hotel, but he was blocking my path.

'So that nice Mr Belcher wants to buy the hotel, eh?' he sneered.

I tried not to look surprised before asking him. 'How did you know?'

'It's my job to know. I'm a reporter, remember?'

I tried to push my way past him, but he held out his arms.

'You won't like that, will you? Being chucked out of your home? But maybe there's something you can do to stop him.'

'How can I stop him?' I asked sarcastically, but desperately wanting to believe that I *could*.

Joe Lowin paused, then leaned his face close to mine. 'If you came up with some money. I mean lots of money.'

'I haven't got lots of money.'

'No, but I have. At least the *Daily News* has. The *Daily News* has got thousands.'

'Why would the *Daily News* give me lots of money?'

'For a bit of information.'

Of course, I had guessed straight away what the 'information' was. I should have told him to push off, there and then. But I didn't, did I.

'I got to thinking,' Joe Lowin was saying, 'this mutant alien monster wotsit. The place it disappeared in was your bedroom, right?'

'Right.'

'So I thought you might have more of an idea where this mutant alien monster wotsit has gone than I have. Right?'

'Right.'

His smile was still a sneer. I'd seen him treat people like dirt, so I knew he wouldn't care much for Gians. And I knew deep down that I shouldn't be trusting anyone who called me 'sonny'. But all I could think about was my broken telescope. That, and mum having to sell the hotel to Moneybags Belcher.

When we passed the office window, Belcher was still sitting there. Mum was on the phone, probably to the bank, I thought. I knew there wasn't a lot of time though. I had to get the money before she signed anything.

'Well, come on, sonny! Open up!'

'You're not going to do anything to him?'

'Of course not.'

'When will I get the money?'

'Look, I can't give you all that money, not without first seeing what's in there, can I? I can't just take your word for it, sonny Jim.'

Ollie was fast asleep at the foot of my bed. He stirred a little when we came in; stretched an arm and then curled up tighter into a ball.

I knew straight away then what a terrible thing I was doing. I had to keep fighting the thoughts in my head so that they said *It's all right Martin. You need the money. Your mum needs the money. You're doing it to help her.*

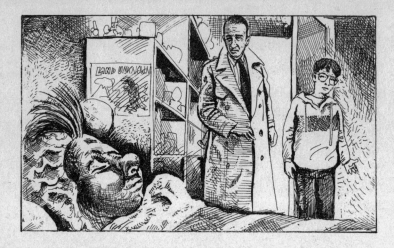

'You're not going to do anything to him.' I was telling Joe Lowin, rather than asking him.

'Eh? No, of course not. Funny looking thing, isn't it?'

'It's a he.'

'Fantastic!'

'He's called Ollie.'

'How do you know?'

'He told us.'

'Cor! He speaks English? Even better! Where's he come from?'

'We found him on the beach.'

'I meant originally.'

'The planet Gia.'

'Never heard of it.'

Joe Lowin was moving towards the door.

'Can I have my money?'

Joe Lowin took the key from my door. He spat one word at me: 'Out!'

I followed him into the corridor. My head was screaming with frightened voices.

'Mr Lowin, I want my money. And I want my key!'

'Sssh! You'll wake it!'

Joe Lowin locked my bedroom door and made off down the corridor.

'Where are you going?'

'I just got to make a phone call to, er...clear the money.'

He was lying. I could see it. Lying through his great ugly face. I stumbled down the stairs after him.

'My money, Mr Lowin, please!'

'Look, sonny. You go out and play. I'll see you later.'

I followed him to the pay phone. Mum came out of the office. 'Martin, come here a moment, will you?'

'Yes, in a minute.'

'Not in a minute, Martin. Now!'

I went.

As she closed the office door behind us, I heard Joe Lowin's voice on the phone. 'We're going to need a cage – and ropes,' he was saying. 'Thick ropes, oh, and chains. I can see the headline now "Gotcha!"'

I felt violently sick.

Moneybags Belcher was nowhere in sight. Mum gave me a big hug. 'Martin, I should be cross...but thank you, thank you, thank you.'

There were tears in her eyes, but happy tears; tears of relief.

'You've certainly got a nerve. You and those girls,' she laughed.

'What are you talking about mum?'

She laughed and gave me another hug. My mind was a whirl. Why wasn't she upset? We were having to sell the hotel to Moneybags Belcher weren't we, for goodness sake?

'It's all right Martin, you can stop pretending. I've worked it all out. Amina's magic tricks, the space monster. They were both your ideas, weren't they? You thought that they might make people curious and want to come and see for themselves, didn't you? And you were right! First I had a call from a group making a booking for a Magic Circle weekend.

They'd read about Amina's amazing tricks in the *Daily News*. And just now I had another call from the Space Trek Fan Club. They read about your space alien in the *Daily News* and they're booking a whole series of group holidays – and they want to launch them with a party here. Tonight! We're going to be packed out for the next month at least.'

My head was swimming. I tried to bring myself to smile, but I couldn't. Through the office window I could see Joe Lowin about to put the phone down.

Mum was going on, '…and so I rang the bank and told them. And the upshot is, thanks to your little jokes and Mr Lowin's pieces in the paper, we don't have to sell the hotel to Mr Belcher after all!'

We don't have to sell the hotel to Mr Belcher after all, I thought.

Ollie! I thought.

I was out of the office and across the hall, mum yelling after me, 'Martin! Martin!'

'Ollie!' I yelled.

Out of the corner of my eye, I saw two familiar figures trotting through the front door: Amina and Jenny. I had no time to stop them now.

I took the stairs two at a time. Joe Lowin had seen me and, leaving the phone dangling, was charging after me. When I got to the top landing something caught my ankle. I crashed onto the floor.

What had caught my ankle was Joe Lowin.

'Let go!' I yelled.

'What do you think you're doing, sonny!'

'Ollie,' I shouted at the top of my voice. 'He's coming! Joe Lowin's coming!'

And he was. I put up my arms to try and stop him, but in no time at all Joe Lowin had clambered over me and was at my bedroom door, key in hand. I scrambled to my feet and Amina grabbed my shoulder.

'What have you done, Martin Rowlands? What have you done?'

Mum, Amina, Jenny and I tumbled into my room after Joe Lowin.

My telescope still lay on the floor, as did my atlas, three dirty socks, a couple of comics and the clothes that Ollie had been wearing. But of Ollie himself there was no sign at all.

Joe Lowin started twitching and then shaking. 'It was there! I saw it. He saw it! Tell 'em sonny Jim!'

'Tell 'em Mr Lowin?'

'About the mutant alien monster wotsit! You said

its name was Mollie or something and it came from another planet—'

'I don't know what you're talking about,' I said, trying to avoid his eyes; trying to avoid Amina's eyes, and Jenny's.

Then Joe Lowin caught sight of the pile of my clothes that Ollie had been wearing.

'This is what it was wearing. These are its clothes.'

My mum was chuckling. Now she hadn't got to sell the Burlington Hotel, she found anything funny. 'Those are Martin's clothes! And I do wish you wouldn't use the floor as a laundry basket, Martin!'

Joe Lowin didn't believe her. '*He* was with me!' He stabbed a tobacco-stained finger in my direction. 'He saw it too!'

Mum carried on chuckling to herself and the more she chuckled, the more Joe Lowin fumed. He turned to look straight down into my eyes. 'Listen sonny Jim, I don't know what stunt you're trying to pull here, but you're not going to get your money until you produce this alien wotsit.'

Amina's eyes grew wide. 'What money?'

'I don't want any money,' I spluttered quickly.

'Changed our tune sonny Jim, haven't we,'

sneered Joe Lowin.

'What money?' asked Amina again. But Joe Lowin took no notice of her. He was shaking with anger. 'I know it's here somewhere – and wherever it is, I'll find it. No one makes fun of Joe Lowin.' He spun round on his heel, sharply, like a soldier, and left.

'Phew!' said mum. And laughed, again. 'We can stop these little games now, don't you think Martin?'

When she had gone, Amina and Jenny slammed the door and started marching towards me. I tried to back off, but the wall wasn't far enough away.

I couldn't look into their faces.

'What games, Martin?'

'What *money*, Martin? Martin!'

'I don't know,' I mumbled. I was trying to think how I could talk my way out of it.

'You pathetic creature, Martin Rowlands,' Amina's voice was full of contempt. 'Ollie trusted us and you told on him! For money!'

'No…it wasn't like that!'

'And you haven't even got the guts to own up to it!'

I couldn't breathe. That familiar feeling. My lungs were locked.

'We…I…to stop Belcher. Getting…hotel,' I panted,

before getting the inhaler into my mouth.

'Leave him, Amina!' ordered Jenny.

Amina stomped away towards the door. 'We've got to find Ollie. Come on!' she said to Jenny.

Jenny looked from the door to me and back again. 'Are you all right, Martin?' she asked me.

I nodded.

Amina was already half way down the corridor. 'Come on, Jenny!' she called. 'The traitor can take care of himself.'

Jenny looked hard at me and shook her head. 'Oh Martin, you are an *idiot*!' she said. But she sounded more sad than angry.

Then she dashed for the door and I heard her and Amina's footsteps crashing down the stairs.

It wasn't a bad attack. I sat up on the bed trying to collect my thoughts. In the distance I heard the piercing wail of a police car. It got steadily louder, until it stopped. Outside the hotel.

I ran to the window. Just as I had thought. Joe Lowin was jumping up and down waving his arms about. He'd called in the police to search for Ollie. I picked up the pile of clothes that Ollie had been wearing and threw them on. I knew there was only one thing I could do.

I skidded round to the front of the hotel on my bike.

'Those girls! See them? They're friends of his!'

'Friends of the alien?' asked the policeman.

'No, friends of that little monster Rowlands!'

'Is he an alien, too?'

'No!' If Joe Lowin had been an engine he would've blown a gasket by now. I rang the two-tone horn on my bike. Lowin and the policeman turned round.

'There he is!' yelled Joe Lowin.

'Who?' asked the policeman.

'The alien you stupid—'

I didn't wait to find out precisely what Joe Lowin called the police officer. I pedalled as hard as I could, all the time fighting for my breath. I weaved in and out of the pillars underneath the prom, then, pushing hard on the pedals and standing right out of the saddle, I got up the hill and into the town proper.

But they were gaining on me all the time. There were traffic lights ahead and I had to turn left – into the High Street. It was a wide road, a fast road. I'd got no breath left. There was a giant hammer thump-thumping away in my chest. I knew it. Stupid asthma. Stupid, stupid asthma. I was going to collapse at any minute. The wailing was right on my tail.

I turned back towards the front. Suddenly a great big yellow removal van drew up in front of me. The way was blocked. I skidded the bike round. Joe Lowin and the policeman came uneasily towards me as if they were trying to catch a dangerous animal. Then out of the corner of my eye I saw two shiny black bollards that marked the new pedestrian precinct. I swung the bike between them. Joe Lowin made a grab for my mudguard, but went sprawling. There was no way the police car could catch me now.

In no time at all, I was back down the hill to the beach. I had no doubt as to where Ollie had gone.

Belcher's factory was quiet. There were a couple of cars in the yard, but neither of them was Belcher's. There was no sign of Ollie and no sign of Amina or Jenny. I leaned my bike up against the fence and tried to think. The space probe was likely to be at the dirtiest spot in the water and Ollie needed to get as close to it as possible to give the call sign. There was no doubt about it. The dirtiest spot must be next to the chemical store where Jenny's dad had worked. I had a quick look round to make sure no one was about, then rushed across the yard to the chemical store.

The door was open. I peered in. My heart missed a beat. I could hear breathing coming from the far corner, I was sure of it.

I tiptoed in. 'Ollie?' I whispered.

'What do *you* want?' A harsh accusing voice; not

Ollie's, but Amina's.

'Have you found him? Is he all right?' I blubbered.

'Yes, we have found him, and no, he's not all right.'

'Did you manage to throw Joe Lowin and the police off?' asked Jenny.

I nodded.

'We saw you. Well done.'

As my eyes began to get used to the murky gloom I saw Ollie. He was curled up asleep. He looked just like he did when we first found him, five days before, except that neither our voices nor our furious shaking of his shoulders seemed to wake him.

'Ollie,' I whispered.

'It's your fault he's like this,' snapped Amina. 'When Ollie had to choose between saving energy for himself or curing Claire and me, he chose to help Claire and me. When you had to choose between saving Ollie or grabbing some easy money, you chose the money. Jenny and I have *found Charley*! But how is Ollie going to get to it now? Southbeach could go up any minute! Ollie will never get back to his space craft!'

I couldn't bear to hear any more from her. I knelt

down and spoke to Ollie. 'Ollie, listen! I'm really sorry!'

I felt something touch my arm. I looked down and saw Ollie's hand.

'Ollie!'

It was deathly quiet in that storeroom as we waited for Ollie to wake up. Then I heard him say, 'Martin? Come on the Gunners!'

'Ollie, wake up!'

But he had gone back to sleep. Curing Amina and Claire; hiding from Joe Lowin, the walk from the hotel to Belcher's factory – it had all taken too much of his energy. His energy! I grabbed Ollie's wrist.

'Martin! What are you doing!' Jenny sounded alarmed.

'Getting that white ball thing. The thing that gives him energy.'

'But we don't know how to work it!'

'We'll do what Ollie does. Put our hands on it and think. Deeply. Remember what he said. *You can do anything if you believe in it enough!*'

'That's right,' said Jenny. 'Believe hard!'

There was a screech of tyres in the yard outside. 'We're going to need to,' I muttered. 'Someone's coming!'

'Go on Ollie,' urged Jenny. 'Disappear! Quick!'

I thought hard about Ollie. How he had told us he trusted us because we believed in him; because we believed in our planet. Our hands surrounded the white ball. I thought, *come on you Gunners*.

At first, it was just a tiny spot of light, like a luminous dot. Then it grew until the whole ball was glowing. It spread like a shaft of sunlight out towards Ollie.

But he didn't disappear. He began to stir. Then he rolled over, sat up and opened his eyes.

'Ollie!'

The glow from the white ball dimmed, sputtered and finally went out.

Then there was a crash behind us, as the door slammed.

'Hey!' yelled Amina, as we heard the key turning in the lock.

I ran to the door. There was a long thin crack in it. I squinted through. Walking away from us was Belcher. He had seen it all.

'Guess who!' I said.

Jenny and Amina left Ollie in the corner and came and peered through the crack with me. We hammered on the door. We pulled at the handle. We yelled: 'Mr Belcher! Please!'

Through the crack I saw Belcher dive into his car, grab his car phone and start to dial. Claire was sitting in the passenger seat.

'What are you doing, dad?'

He was busy with his phone.

'Claire!' I yelled, and thumped like mad on the door.

She looked across. And twigged. 'Dad! You've never locked them in there!'

But Belcher was still busy dialling. Claire reached across to him, grabbed her dad's arm and began trying to wrestle the phone from him.

'Flipping Nora! She's fighting him!' I said. We all pushed our faces up close to the crack.

'Get off Claire! Let go!' shouted Belcher.

'No, I'm not going to let go,' screamed Claire.

The phone fell out of Belcher's hand and fell at Claire's feet.

Then the phone spoke: 'Hello? Which emergency service do you require?'

Belcher made a quick grab for the phone, but Claire looked daggers at him. 'I'm warning you, dad,' she said, 'I'll break it if you try.' She obviously had her foot over it. It sounded funny, her threatening Belcher like this but still calling him 'dad'.

'Hello? Hello?' said the phone.

'Police! Police!' screamed Belcher.

'No!' There was a crack of shattering plastic and then the phone went dead. Claire had meant what she said.

Moneybags Belcher sat there for a moment like a dummy. As if he had suddenly found himself in a world he didn't understand. Like he knew he wasn't in control any more.

'The key please, dad.'

Over in the corner Ollie was clumsying about. Any minute now he's going to drop off to sleep again I thought.

'Hurry! Hurry!' I muttered.

Moneybags Belcher was making one last effort. Trying to be Mr Nice Guy. 'Claire! What do you think you're doing, love? You realise what those kids have done to your old dad? Out of sheer spite they've ruined him!'

'What do you mean?' asked Claire, stepping back a bit from her father.

Don't listen to him, Claire! Don't listen to him! I prayed.

Belcher took an official-looking letter from his pocket. 'This came this morning,' he said. 'It's a court order closing the factory down.' He read a bit of the letter to Claire. 'A sample of water tested by our scientists shows a dangerously high level of toxic material.' He pointed an accusing finger at the locked door. '*They* did that to me! They sneaked down here and got that sample of water. At least now I've got them in there, the police can get them for breaking and entering.' His eyes lit up. 'And who knows, I might even be able to shift the blame for all the muck onto that alien monster thing they've got with them. Eh? That'll teach them to go running to the authorities about a drop of dirty water!'

'It wasn't them who went running to the

authorities about a drop of dirty water, dad,' said Claire quietly.

'Then who did?'

'I did.'

Belcher froze. 'No…Claire!'

'And it isn't a "drop of dirty water", it's polluted and dangerous and it made me and Amina and lots of other people ill!'

'But you're better now love!'

'No thanks to you.'

'But Claire! Listen to me! Everyone chucks their junk into the river and the sea. Why let them pick on me, your old dad?'

'It's not *your* river dad. And it's not your sea. It's everybody's. And everybody's got to look after it. And that includes you!'

'Here, here! Well said old thing!' chirruped a voice beside me. Ollie had sneaked up and was watching the proceedings with interest. Claire's outburst seemed to have renewed his energy.

Moneybags Belcher was looking at Claire as if he was looking at a stranger. 'I–I didn't know you thought like that,' he mumbled.

'Well I do,' said Claire frostily. 'Perhaps I should

have said so before, instead of always sitting about in the car, trying to pretend that what you did had nothing to do with me.'

'Claire! What are you saying? What has happened to you?' It was odd, but it sounded as if Belcher *really* wanted to know.

'Do you remember, the other day, at the door of Martin's mum's hotel when you grabbed Amina? You said to Martin and Amina and Jenny, "Do you kids really believe you can change anything?" Well they've changed me, dad.'

'What do you mean? They changed you?'

'They kept coming until they'd got their evidence. They didn't give up. And I thought, if they can care that much about the Earth, so can I. Give me the key.'

'If I've lost you Claire, I've lost everything...' blubbered Belcher.

'Don't be so over-dramatic, dad,' answered Claire, firmly. 'Of course you haven't lost me. Look, if Amina, Jenny and Martin can change things, so can you. It's not too late to join us.'

Perhaps for the first time in his life, Moneybags Belcher was lost for words.

'Now,' said Claire, 'can I have the key, please?'

Like a man hypnotised, Belcher put his hand into his pocket, took out the key and gave it to Claire.

As she turned it in the lock, I could already hear the wailing of police sirens as they approached the factory.

Ollie was shaking Claire's hand. 'Well done!' he exclaimed.

'Ollie! Come on! There isn't much time,' yelled Jenny urgently.

I could see Joe Lowin and a number of police officers getting out of cars and heading our way. Belcher was making his way towards them. Ollie ran out of the door towards the sea, then stumbled and fell.

'Grab him!' I yelled. Jenny, Amina, Claire and I took an arm and a leg each and headed over down the bank to the water's edge.

'Quick! This way!' I heard Belcher shouting. Then again more quietly, 'follow me!' I glanced round. Belcher was deliberately leading Joe Lowin and the police *away* from us!

'Don't worry Ollie,' said Amina. 'There's *five* of us helping you now. Claire's dad's joined the team!'

'Charley! Charley!' called Ollie.

'Charley!' warbled a computer-like voice near our feet. There, half-hidden under a rock that was stained a bright yellow from the factory waste was the Gian space probe, the shape of a shell, little red lights beaming from within. Suddenly, it began to shine brilliantly with a fierce strobe effect.

'Quick!' said Ollie, 'there's only a few seconds! It's about to blow!'

We dropped him into the water and he bent down to the probe. Then he seemed to stroke the space probe.

'OK, old chap, we'll soon have you fixed,' he said to the probe, like he was a vet talking to a sick animal. Carefully, he put his hand inside the probe and felt around. The probe let out a screech, like the squeal of brakes on a car.

'No!' I yelled, sure that the probe was going to blow. But the glow slowly faded away. Ollie pulled out a small object, about the size of a cork.

'Ah-hah!' said Ollie, 'just in time,' and he staggered out of the water towards us, then collapsed at our feet.

The fierce light and the squeal had brought Joe Lowin and the police running.

'Let's get it!' roared Joe Lowin.

'No!' screamed Belcher, 'let him go!'

'I've got to go,' said Ollie. He fumbled in his wrist-computer thing and took out the pearl-white sphere. 'This is for you,' he said.

'Oh Ollie…' said Amina, 'you…you *nincomploop!* Thank you!'

'Thank *you*,' said Ollie. 'Thank you all.'

We all wanted to say things to Ollie, like *Good bye*, and *Don't worry there won't be any earth warps not if we have anything to do with it*, but none of us said anything. We didn't seem able to get the words out.

Ollie stepped into the sea and turned to wave. 'Believe in your planet!' he called.

There was a scuffle behind us as Joe Lowin, making one last desperate sprint to catch Ollie, was felled by an impressive rugby tackle from Claire's dad.

Then everybody stopped and listened, even the policemen. A strange, haunting tune came drifting over the waves. It was being whistled up by Ollie. He was calling up his space craft. It rose slowly out of the water, like a submarine, graceful and curved like a bird, just as I had seen it through my telescope five nights ago. With a final wave, Ollie climbed in. Then the space craft rose up and, climbing higher and higher through a great arc, finally disappeared from sight.

Everyone walked back up the beach in silence. The only noise was the crackle of the police officers' radios.

Claire and her dad got into their car.

'See you, Claire!' said Amina.

Claire nodded.

'Er…thank you, Mr Belcher,' said Jenny awkwardly. 'For stopping him—' she nodded in the direction of Joe Lowin, who was sitting on the pavement, rubbing his bruises.

'Yeah,' Claire's dad shrugged. His mind seemed miles away. He and Claire went off with the policeman.

Joe Lowin hobbled over. 'Now you kids,' he began, 'how would you all like to earn some money? Your story, in an exclusive for the *Daily News*.'

'No thanks,' said Jenny. 'Our exclusive story is going to the *Southbeach Gazette*.'

Joe Lowin went red. 'Don't be daft!' he yelled.

We walked away.

'I've got lots of money!' yelled Joe Lowin. 'Come back!'

We didn't.

And neither did he.

He left the hotel that afternoon. His bosses weren't exactly pleased that he had been scooped by the *Southbeach Gazette*. They didn't give him the sack, but he was demoted and given the most junior job on the paper: they put him in charge of the 'Spot the Ball' competition.

'I've been keeping a diary every day!' Jenny told Sarah Brightly. 'Great,' said Sarah, 'we'll write a special report for the *Gazette,* together!'

I kept quiet about my diary. There were some things in it which I didn't want...well, splashed all over the *Gazette* for a start. Besides, I was already planning to write up the events of the last few days myself, not as a report, but as a *story*.

Epilogue: Day five plus five

I walked along the sea front towards the fishing
boats where we had first seen Ollie. I'd arranged to
meet Jenny, Amina and Claire there.

'Hell-oo-ee! Martin!' Mrs Wimpy hailed me. She and Old Granny Grant were sitting in one of the big shelters on the promenade. 'Are there any space ships landing today?'

'No,' I called back, 'I don't think so.'

'What a pity! I've enjoyed it all so much,' she beamed.

Since she had stood up to Old Granny Grant over staying put in the hotel, she had become a different person. It was odd. When I thought about it, since day one, everybody had changed a bit. Mum and Chef were happy and busy now that the hotel was getting booked up; Jenny's dad had a new job; Claire's dad was backing the 'Clean Up Southbeach' campaign.

And Jenny, Amina, Claire and me? I think we all felt a bit different somehow. That was Ollie for you.

On the beach, Amina said, 'It's funny you know. I miss him.'

'I never did get to say thank you,' added Claire.

'I don't think any of us did,' I said.

'Do you think he'll ever come back?' asked Jenny.

'Do you think he'll need to?' asked Amina.

'Oh yes,' I said.

They all looked at me. 'Why?'

'He'll need an "Ollie" day!'

It took a moment or two to sink in and then all three of them started rolling around clutching their stomachs and groaning loudly.

Well, you can change a lot of things, but you'll never change my jokes.

They'll always be really brilliant.

Earth Warp

Have you seen this range of resources for Earth Warp?

storybook, audio cassette, photocopymasters and software.

Storybooks available in packs of 5 only
0 563 35399 6

Photocopymasters
0 563 35400 3

Software BBC B/B+/M128
 0 582 222852 2

Software Archimedes
0 582 22851 4

Software RML Nimbus
0 582 22961 8

To order any of the above, use your termly order form.
Alternatively, send a cheque, payable to BBC Educational
Publishing (include £1.50 postage and packing) with details
of title, quantity and ISBN to:

BBC Educational Publishing, PO Box 234, Wetherby,
West Yorkshire, LS23 7EU.

To confirm prices telephone 0937 541001 between 10.00am
and 4.00pm or see your termly BBC order form.